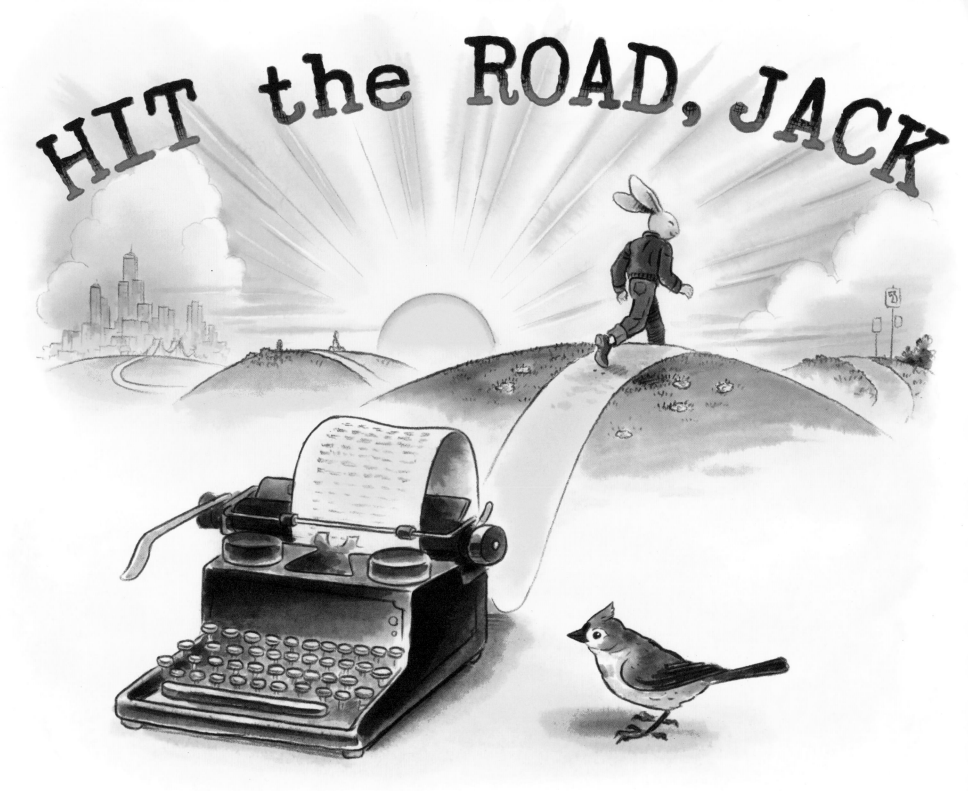

HIT the ROAD, JACK

By **Robert Burleigh**   Illustrated by R

Abrams Books for Young Readers

New York

To Mark Burleigh, with love

—R.B.

For my parents, who taught
me to love the open road

—R.M.

The illustrations in this book were made with
watercolor and pencil crayon.

Cataloging-in-Publication Data has been applied for
and may be obtained from the Library of Congress.
ISBN: 978-1-4197-0399-7

Book design by Ross MacDonald and Chad W. Beckerman

Printed and bound in China
10 9 8 7 6 5 4 3 2 1

Abrams Books for Young Readers are available at
special discounts when purchased in quantity for
premiums and promotions as well as fundraising
or educational use. Special editions can also
be created to specification. For details, contact
specialsales@abramsbooks.com or the address below.

ABRAMS
THE ART OF BOOKS SINCE 1949
115 West 18th Street
New York, NY 10011
www.abramsbooks.com

Hey, Jack! Skedaddle! Gotta hop!
Vamoose! Take off and go!
Nose is itching, ears are twitching,
Come on! Get with the flow!
Time to see the road unwind
And feel the wind blow free.
"Hello, America! Here I come,
From sea to shining sea!"

Bye-bye to jam-packed city streets,
So long to New York nights.
Zip the backpack. Lock the door.
Turn out all the lights.
Next stop, 42nd Street,
Where Greyhound buses load,
'Cause you hear the old voice calling:
"Hey, Jack, hit the road."

Moon-glow on the Hudson,
Philly in the dawn,
Throw kisses to the Liberty Bell,
Hot coffee, and you're gone.
Truck it, train it, bike it, hike it,
Hoist your thumb up, rain or snow.
Tonight you'll be in Boston town,
Then on to Buffalo.

From woodsy Pennsylvania,
To Pittsburgh's smoky gray.
What's certain is tomorrow
Won't be lookin' like today.
Ohio's hills are green and fine.
No matter—don't unpack.
The road, the road, the road, the road . . .
You gotta hit it, Jack.

Hey-hey to Cleveland Willie,
High fives for Detroit Lou,
A hug for Hannah Hoosier, Jack,
But you're just passing through.
Catch some shut-eye on the fly,
Count headlights, one by one,
Then wake to see the Windy City,
Rising with the sun.

Go bopping down South Halsted Street.
Where's the action? What's the news?
Fill the jukebox up with dimes,
Slip on your dancin' shoes.
Gaze up at glass and steel—but yo—
There's lots more landscape yet.
The road's still calling, "Jack Jack Jack,"
And so you gotta get.

Here's to early morning,
When the air is tinged with blue,
And everything's beginning,
And the whole world calls to you.
The open sky, the first deep breath—
What else does Jackson need?
Just clouds that roll on overhead,
Like puffs of tumbleweed.

In train yards thick with rambling rose,
You hop a rusty freight,
A free ride to wherever—
Go Jack! Don't be late.
Past cornstalks waving, Jackie-boy!
And rows of gold soybeans,
Now over the Mississippi,
Flowing south to New Orleans.

Sterling City, Oxford Junction,
West Branch, Victor, Blair,
The road goes this- and that-a-way,
Never asking where.
Lone Tree, Newton, Oskaloosa,
Redfield, Poplar Bluff,
A thousand names fly by—but Jack,
There'll never be enough.

The wind against the windshield,
The smell of rubber burning,
An old tune on the radio,
The click of wheels a-turning.
Into the Great Plains, growing dark,
A farm, a twinkling light,
While the moon plays whoopsie-doopsie
With the blackness of the night.

Concrete highways, asphalt byways,
Gravel, mud, or dust—
It's all the same to you, old buddy,
Westward ho or bust!
The presidents on Rushmore wink,
"Here's lookin' at you, Jack."
But you keep cruising, sailing on,
And simply grin right back.

Snatch naps on cold park benches.
Catch zzz's in bus depots,
Or barns with sweetly smelling hay—
Easy as it goes.
You miss a meal once or twice,
You're broke—but well, so what?
'Cause money's only something, Jack,
That gets you in a rut.

Zooming through the Rockies,
Past Denver, mile-high,
Where the road winds ever upward,
Until it meets the sky.
You stand upon a snowy peak,
And gaze down from above,
At the never-ending scenery
Of this country that you love.

Check out the billboards as you pass:
FRIED LIZARDS—HAVE A TREAT!
OLD DINO BONES! A THREE-EYED CALF!
DOC QUACKER'S CURE FOR TIRED FEET!
WITCH'S CAVERN! BRONCO RIDES!
YOUR FORTUNE TOLD! THE BUSY BEE!
Ah, the road signs, left and right,
That read like poetry!

The folks you meet along the way,
You'd like to hear from each.
Everyone's got a story—
But you've got a coast to reach.
There's Lil the waitress, Mac the miner,
Juanita, Herb, and Cowboy Jake.
"A burger? Not for me," you say,
"Just make mine carrot cake!"

Over the salt flats, on and on,
The horizon thick with reds,
And mesas looming far, far off,
Like carved-out giants' heads.
An eagle soars, a butterfly drifts,
Bright desert flowers bloom.
They're singing your song, Jack, my friend,
"Hey, World, gimme room!"

The road's your schoolhouse-on-the-move,
But now the road winds down.
You're at the blue Pacific—
San Francisco town!
Keep those tired legs pumping,
To where your pals all wait,
And wave good-bye to the setting sun
Beyond the Golden Gate.

You'd like to stay forever,
But something whispers, "Hop!"
There's just one rule
For guys like you, Jack:
NEVER, NEVER STOP.

And so it's time to start again,
For one more episode
Of the story that you're living
Titled "Hey, Jack, Hit the Road" . . .
The story that you're living
Titled "Hey, Jack, Hit the Road."

WHO WAS JACK?

There once was a man named Jack who was a writer. But he was a traveler, too!

Jack thought traveling was a marvelous adventure, especially traveling across America. He and his friends took long trips across the country, stopping along the way to gaze at glorious sunsets, camp in the mountains, explore the big cities, and meet people who lived out in the country and in small towns. It didn't much matter where they were going. Jack and his friends just liked being "on the road."

And along the way, Jack wrote! He wanted what he wrote to feel as free and loose and wild and crazy as a jackrabbit hopping and bopping along. He wrote about what he saw and felt, and often his stories were more like poems.

Jack Kerouac (that was his real full name) was always trying to make his writing fun to read. One day, you may even read his most famous book. It's called—you guessed it!—*On the Road*. And here's something else: He wrote his book on a single long roll of unbroken paper—so it unrolled before him, just like the road itself!

—Robert Burleigh

NEW YORK! CLEVELA BOSTON! COLUMBUS CHICA SAN F FRESNO!